Cindy's demanding day

More Books from Macy & JC

TALES OF A TEENAGE ALIEN HUMAN HYBRID

The Alien's Daughter

The Hybrid Challenge

COMING SOON

The Human Complication

SILVER CITY PRINCESSES

Cindy's Demanding Day

COMING SOON

A Challenge for Maree

Risa's Secret Weapon

SILVER CITY PRINCESS STORIES

BOOK ONE

MACY MORROWS

JC MORROWS

S&G PUBLISHING

Cindy's Demanding Day

S&G Publishing, Knoxville, TN
www.sgpublish.com

This book is a work of fiction. Names, characters, places, and incidents are either products of the author's imagination or used fictitiously. Any similarity to actual people, organizations, and/or events is purely coincidental

S&G Publishing, Knoxville, TN
www.sgpublish.com

Scripture quotations are from the Holy Bible (KJV)

Library of Congress Cataloging-in-Publication Data

Morrows, Macy & Morrows, JC

Cindy's Demanding Day / Macy Morrows, JC Morrows

1. Middle Grade / Fiction / Religious / Christian / Fairy Tales. 2. Middle Grade / Fiction / Fantasy / Fairy Tales. 3. Middle Grade / Fiction / Fantasy. 4. Middle Grade / Fiction / Science Fiction & Fantasy.

ISBN: 978-1948733946

2019931012

First Edition: 2019

PRINTED AND BOUND IN THE UNITED STATES OF AMERICA

For Grandma

"Here's to love laughter and HAPPILY ever after"

- unknown

Chapter One

Cindy paused for a moment as she looked up at the familiar window, daydreaming about the old-fashioned palace that was etched and painted with obvious care into the glass.

The scene was so beautifully designed, she could easily imagine herself sitting by a window in one of the shining silvery towers, or perhaps running through the clear meadow beneath the shimmering palace that was filled with delicate carved flowers.

And it's in their bathroom.

The idea was almost ridiculous to her. . . to have so much money, you would put something so beautiful in the bathroom. It almost felt wrong.

Almost.

But Cindy had to admit, if she had the sort of money this family obviously did, she would probably be just as likely to surround herself with beautiful things, even in the bathroom.

This house was one of her favorite places in the city to clean. And since they cleaned the house every week, even though the family who lived there was not very messy at all, she was able to enjoy it often.

One reason I don't even mind drawing bathroom duty.

There were so many beautiful things throughout the house to enjoy looking at while she worked.

Of course, this particular window was probably wasted since she knew this was their son's bathroom.

Could a boy truly appreciate the beauty of such a delicate and intricate scene?

Probably not.

They cleaned many houses where boys lived, and it was all Cindy could do not to giggle when she thought about how the boys' bathrooms were almost always messier—and a lot smellier—than the girls' bathrooms.

But I would appreciate it.

Of course, the same was true of most of the girls who worked for her stepmother too. They went about their job without paying a bit of attention to the beauty they were surrounded by every day.

Cindy allowed herself a moment to think about it. . . and to dream of what her house would look like, if she lived in one like this.

If she could, she would have many of the windows etched with beautiful scenes like this one.

In rooms where people enjoyed looking out upon beautifully landscaped lawns, she would have a large, clear glass window, along with smaller ones on either side with intricate designs etched into the glass.

And she would have. . .

A sound from down the hall

distracted her.

She knew it would not be a good idea to draw attention to herself—and daydreams were for free time, not work time—so she sighed and went back to scrubbing.

Just as she reached up to flush the suds that had gathered in the bowl as she worked, a harsh voice sounded from behind her.

"Cindy, haven't you finished yet?" The sound of anger in her stepmother's words caused Cindy to jump and she nearly dropped the brush she was holding into the white, porcelain bowl in front of her.

Her stepmother let out a huff of

annoyance at Cindy's clumsiness. "Oh, for goodness sake. You need to hurry up. The rest of the girls are nearly done now. You are holding us up."

Cindy didn't bother to tell her that she was already finished with the bathroom. She only nodded her head and made a point of scrubbing quickly against the porcelain until the hard taps of the high-heels her stepmother was so fond of sounded behind her.

How does she even walk in those crazy shoes?

The thought came to Cindy just about every time she heard their harsh tapping against a floor, but she never dared ask, knowing her stepmother had no patience for questions—especially questions from Cindy.

She also knew her stepmother would be angry if she had to wait for her, so Cindy quietly stood, took one last look at the window in front of her, and then turned to gather up her cleaning supplies.

Moving quickly and quietly through the house, she made her way to the back stairs—the servant's staircase—and hurried down them, careful not to brush against the white walls on either side of her.

When she arrived in the back hallway where they were to gather, she was surprised to see only one other girl waiting there.

Didn't she say all the other girls were nearly finished? Shouldn't they be lining up already—or at least coming down the stairs by now?

She didn't say it out loud though. Asking questions never seemed to go as well for her in real life as it felt like it should when the questions popped into her head.

Chapter Two

While the van sped through the city, Cindy took advantage of her chance to do nothing but sit and watch it go by. Silver City really was a beautiful place to live.

It was the one thing that made her

life bearable. As the youngest daughter—actually the step-daughter, she reminded herself—of Mistress Ward, and the youngest maid at Magical Maids Cleaning Services, her days were full.

Every day as they drove out to the jobs and then back to the manor where Cindy had grown up, a place that had never felt quite like home since her dad had passed away, Cindy had the chance to look out the window and do nothing but daydream.

It was pretty much the only time she had... to daydream. . . or do nothing at all, for that matter.

The other girls who worked for her stepmother got days off each week. They even took vacations. All in all, they worked on about a dozen houses each week.

Cindy worked every day on more than a dozen houses. She never had a day off. She never asked for one. She knew better than to ask.

There were no days off for her. Even going home meant work. At home she was expected to help their small staff take care of the manor, and then to do whatever her stepmother and her two step-sisters required of her. Most of the time it wasn't too bad.

It wasn't that Cindy really minded. She was mostly happy to take care of the home where she had so many wonderful memories with her father.

It was more that she never really felt

like her stepmother or step-sisters thought of her as family.

They certainly don't treat me like family.

They definitely hadn't since the Magical Maids Cleaning Service had taken off.

In the beginning, it had been kind of fun. The four of them had worked together until her stepmother could afford to hire more girls.

It had felt like she was important, like she was a part of their little unit, and she was helping her stepmother to achieve her own dream.

But then her two step-sisters had stopped helping out. And Cindy had thought she could too, but she'd come home from school and her stepmother had been waiting for her.

She had never gotten the chance to stop.

And then her stepmother and step-sisters had started expecting her to work at home too. But by then she no longer felt like part of their family.

With a little sigh, she shrugged and turned her attention back to the city. It was quickly passing and she was wasting her daydreaming time on what-ifs and never-would-be's.

She was not the only girl who sighed as they drove by the palace. And who could blame them.

The girls might not notice beautiful things in the houses they clean, but they certainly noticed the beauty of the palace.

Or maybe it's just the prince they're thinking of.

But Cindy wasn't thinking of the prince as she looked up at the beautiful expanse of white marble that formed the imposing palace of Silver City.

Or not really. . . she did think about how lucky he was to have such a privileged life, to have the kind of freedom he must have.

To think. . . he could do anything, go anywhere. It must be wonderful.

She sighed a little as she looked back at what she imagined to be a perfect place to live.

The palace sat atop a hill so high, it

was practically a mountain. A long, winding road curved up and around the hill, disappearing somewhere near the impressive front gates, so all that you really saw was the palace and a wide stretch of perfect, green grass.

At night, the lights of the palace could be seen from almost everywhere in the city. It was a bright, shining beacon of warmth and welcome.

And when they had parties, there were even more lights, and fireworks, and. . . well, Cindy couldn't quite imagine what the inside of the palace was like during a party, but she was sure it would be better than any party she had ever been to.

Every time there was a special

occasion or a holiday, something big enough for the royal family to contract extra help, her stepmother put in a bid.

Obviously she dreamed about visiting the palace just as much as the girls in her employ, even if it were just to clean it.

She had never yet managed to get the coveted contract, even though Cindy knew she had made some of her bids ridiculously low.

Perhaps some of the other companies do that too.

It made sense. There was nothing more prestigious than being chosen to cater a party at the palace, or even to clean for it.

Chapter Three

Main street was crowded, people rushing past her from both sides, when Cindy turned onto it from the small side street where the van had dropped her off.

They had barely left town when

Mistress Ward's cell phone had rung. Everyone had been able to hear the shrieks coming from whoever had called her. Cindy was pretty sure she knew who was on the other end of the phone line.

One of my dear step-sisters, no doubt.

She couldn't help but feel a little cheated that her peaceful ride home had been interrupted.

But at least she wouldn't have to go home right away to deal with whatever had upset her step-sister.

After several minutes of shrill speech that made Cindy's ears hurt, even though the phone was several feet away, her stepmother had told the driver to stop and let Cindy out.

Then she had given Cindy a long list of instructions to deliver before she could come home.

She had barely stepped out of the van before the door had shut behind her and the van was moving down the road away from her, sending up a cloud of dust in their hurry.

Cindy was in no hurry now though, and since she was safely out of her stepmother's hearing, she laughed about it, knowing that her stepmother would still have to deal with her step-sister when she arrived home. And by the sound of things, it would not be an easy task.

That voice on the other end of the cell

phone could only have been Madeline.

Not only did she have a shriek that could easily have been heard across the phone line and the space between Cindy and her stepmother, but as the oldest, Madeline expected everyone to cater to her every whim, whether they were a servant or not.

No sooner had Cindy turned toward the town, than someone slammed into her, knocking her to the ground.

Her hands and knees hit the sidewalk hard, and the list skittered away from her, dancing along the ground in the breeze.

She didn't have time to think about anything other than capturing the list that was already several feet away, and moving quickly.

She pushed herself to her feet and took off after the list, colliding again with the boy who had knocked her down just a few seconds ago.

He had taken off after the escaping piece of paper at the same time she had.

Fortunately, he snatched the list before it could get too far. His fingers closed around it and his face split into a triumphant smile as he turned back to her.

"Got it!"

Cindy stood there for a few seconds, looking at the boy who acted as though he had saved the day by capturing a runaway paper, only seconds after knocking into her. . . twice.

The boy looked like he was the same age as Cindy, but he was much taller than the boys in her grade at school. He must come from a tall family.

He was also handsome—in a messy kind of way. His dark hair was standing up in all directions, not like it had been styled that way on purpose, but more like it was wind blown or just messy.

He wore a crooked smile. It was one that was full of warmth, so much so that it lit up his whole face with a joy that came from a carefree sort of childhood.

She decided right then and there that he could not possibly have knocked her down on purpose, or because he was not being careful.

He must have been in a hurry to get

where he was going, and had simply not seen her.

And well, he had sort of rescued the paper that had blown out of her hands.

Chapter Four

With a little flourish of his hand and a very formal bow, he handed over the paper.

"I believe I knocked this out of your hand, Miss." His crooked smile turned into a crooked grin. "I am very sorry for knocking you down."

Cindy was surprised to realize that she wanted to laugh. There might be a hint of apology in his crooked grin, but he really did not look at all sorry.

She shrugged and decided to let him off the hook. "No harm done. I'm just fine, and you rescued my list." She smiled and took the list he was holding out to her.

"Pleased to be of service, milady." He stood and his smile widened, revealing a small gap between two of his bottom teeth.

She started to say something else, just as her name sounded from behind her.

"Cindy! Hey, I thought that was you."

Isabelle was cruising along on her little motorized scooter.

She had nearly reached them when Cindy turned to see that the young man was heading off quickly in the opposite direction.

She started to call out, but it was easy to see he was already far enough away that he very likely would not hear her.

With a shake of her head, Cindy turned toward her friend. Isabelle came to a stop about a foot from Cindy, her backpack bouncing a little as she put one foot down on the sidewalk.

“Who was that? He certainly left in a hurry.”

Cindy shook her head as she answered. “I didn't catch his name.”

"Oh." Isabelle watched with Cindy at the young man's back as he got farther away from them. "I did not mean to scare him off."

Cindy shook her head again. "You didn't." A few seconds later, she added, "I don't think so, anyway." Then she shook her head again as she laughed. "It has to be the oddest encounter I've had in some time."

"Really?" Isabelle looked over at her friend, lifting one of her narrow eyebrows in curiosity.

Cindy laughed again before answering. "Yeah. First, he rammed into me and knocked me down. Then he goes after the list I'm supposed to deliver and makes it seem like he pulled off this big rescue or something."

"List? What list?" Isabelle sounded less curious and more concerned now.

Cindy shook her head, ignoring the question, and went on with her description.

"He actually bowed to me when he gave me back the paper. Can you believe that?" She looked over at Isabelle, watching her friend's face as she debated what to say next. "Doesn't that strike you as a bit odd?"

"I suppose." Isabelle's voice was neutral when she answered, but something in her expression told Cindy she was not ready to let go of the list business.

"He was cute though, huh?" Not that

Isabelle payed attention much to how cute boys were, unless they were in one of her books anyway.

"I do not believe I saw him well enough to know. Now, tell me about this list, Cindy. Is it something else your stepmother has given you to do?"

Cindy didn't answer. She just turned and started down the sidewalk again. After a few seconds, Isabelle appeared beside her, coasting along on her scooter.

Chapter Five

Cindy hurried along beside Isabelle, who didn't say anything for nearly two blocks. When she did, it was just what Cindy expected. . . what Isabelle usually had to say whenever Cindy's stepmother gave her more to do.

"This is ridiculous. How can she keep

giving you more things to do? How exactly are you supposed to get this done, with everything else you already do?"

When Isabelle glared at her, Cindy only shrugged her shoulders in answer. She could hear the anger in her friend's voice. She appreciated the concern, but she also knew there was nothing she could do about any of it.

When her stepmother wanted something done, there was no arguing with her.

Isabelle huffed. "Please tell me you see how ridiculous this all is. You barely have time to breathe, much less to do something she could just as well do herself."

Cindy just shrugged again. She knew it was ridiculous for her stepmother to keep adding little tasks to her daily list that anyone else could have done.

For that matter, Isabelle was right. Her stepmother could easily do most of them, and much quicker, too. But Cindy also knew there was no point in arguing.

"Somehow, I must find a way to do them." Thinking of her stepmother's anger, she doubled her pace. Isabelle kept up easily, gliding along on her little motorized scooter.

Cindy had always wanted one of the little scooters, especially given how far they lived from town, but had never dared ask for one. She only ever asked for things she could not possibly do without—and even then, it did not always go well.

Concern filling her voice now, Isabelle spoke up again, likely only now realizing that Cindy was going to complete her errand no matter what.

“You can borrow my scooter. I am going to the library and it is certainly close enough to walk.”

“Truly?” Cindy tried to keep the eagerness out of her voice. She had driven the scooter before, and she knew just how much quicker she would arrive with the added speed. “You wouldn't mind?”

“Truly. I would not mind.” Isabelle answered, unconsciously correcting to her usual perfect grammar.

Cindy hid her smile. Her friend never changed.

"Thank you, Isabelle. You are the best friend I have." She didn't finish the thought; Isabelle was also the only friend she had.

She leaned in to give Isabelle a quick hug. Isabelle smiled as she leaned to return her friend's hug.

"Best friend or not, I am simply trying to keep you out of trouble. You know you don't have time enough for everything you already have to do."

Isabelle laughed as soon as she said it, making up for the sting of her words, and Cindy laughed in reply.

Then Isabelle was stepping off the scooter and moving aside so that Cindy could step on.

"I'll be at the library for hours. Just bring it back there when you're done." A moment later, she added, "or would it be better for you to ride it all the way home? I can always come by when I'm done and pick it up."

Cindy nearly replied with a yes. Having the scooter for the ride home would be such a joy and a blessing. But the thought of her stepmother's reaction stopped her, and she shook her head.

If her stepmother thought Cindy had a scooter to help her do things quicker, she might give her even more things to do.

"I'm not sure that would be the best idea. I'll just bring it by the library when

I'm back this way."

"Are you sure? I can easily come by to get it later." Isabelle was clearly trying to help, and Cindy was sure she was trying to decide if she should insist her friend keep the scooter for the ride home.

"Trust me. It would not be a good idea to bring this home. It would look like I have plenty of time to do even more things."

She knew she sounded annoyed now —she could hear it in the clipped, tight tone of her own voice.

She smiled and hugged her friend again. "I'll be back before you know it."

Isabelle still looked unsure, but she didn't argue. "Well, all right. If you are certain. . ."

"I am." Cindy smiled again. Isabelle finally turned to head towards the library.

Cindy wasted no time in turning the scooter towards the shop in town where she was meant to drop off some notes for the dressmaker.

There was some sort of big social event coming up, and her step-sisters were having new dresses made up just for the occasion.

Of course they are.

Cindy knew she shouldn't exactly be surprised, but it still hurt a little that no one had mentioned having a dress made for her.

Chapter Six

Cindy stood in line for a very long time waiting to speak with the dressmaker.

By the time she got a chance to speak to the young woman behind the counter, who looked as if she'd barely had time to crawl out of bed before rushing to work that day and would likely not get to crawl back to bed until late in the night, the shop was getting ready to close for the evening.

“It's a good thing you got here when you did. I remember these dresses. We've already started on them.”

Panic filled Cindy's chest and closed off her throat. Her stepmother would find a way to blame this on her somehow.

What will I do? How can I. . .

She did not get the chance to finish her thought.

The young woman had clearly been reading the list because she looked up from it and gave Cindy a tired smile.

"The good news is, there's nothing here that will cause a problem. And we should still have them ready for the fitting appointment you've already made." She started to walk around the counter, looking at Cindy as she did.

"Neither of the dresses is for you, are they?"

"No. Why?" In her relief, Cindy answered without really thinking—having only half heard the young woman's question.

She shook her head as she answered. "No reason, really. It's just that I know the dresses. Neither one would flatter you in the slightest." Her voice was all business, but Cindy was not at all sure how she should answer.

Should she tell the young woman she was not having a dress made or just nod and leave the store? She didn't have the chance to make the decision though.

"Are we making one for you?"

"No, you're not." Cindy headed for the door, trying to sound a little bored as she answered, like she'd heard her step-sister do a hundred times.

"Shame." She followed Cindy toward the front door as she talked.

"I know so many styles that would look great on you." When Cindy only nodded, she went on. "You come to me when you need a dress made. I'll make sure it's stunning."

Cindy mumbled something like "sure" as she moved through the doorway and out onto the street.

The young woman called out one more time as Cindy walked to the borrowed scooter. "And don't worry. We'll have these ready in time. Have a good evening."

With that, the door clicked shut and Cindy stepped onto Isabelle's scooter.

She stopped the scooter at the bottom of the library steps about ten seconds before Isabelle came walking down them.

"Your timing is perfect, Cindy. How

did you do that?"

Cindy laughed. "Not on purpose, I promise. The dress store was crazy busy. They were getting ready to close by the time I actually got to talk to someone."

"Goodness. That does not sound good."

"I know, right? And they've already started working on the dresses. I was almost too late."

Isabelle's expression mirrored what Cindy had felt earlier, so much so that she was grateful the young woman at the dress shop had not been looking at her when she'd told Cindy the same thing she'd just told her friend.

If I had looked at her like that, she might have worried I was going to faint or something.

"Were you too late with the list, then?"

"Thankfully, no." Cindy sighed before going on. "Can you imagine how much trouble I would've been in if I had been too late?"

"It does not bear thinking of." Then the fire came back into Isabelle's voice. "Though all of this worry and stress could have been avoided if your stepmother had just picked up a phone."

Cindy laughed. No one would ever guess just how fierce Isabelle could be when it came to defending her friends.

"But she didn't, and now she doesn't have to." Cindy smiled and held up a hand. "No, seriously. It's done, and it's late, and I had better get home."

Isabelle sighed. "Let me give you a ride. . ." She rushed on when Cindy started to protest. ". . . at least part of the way."

When Cindy didn't give in, she pushed a little more. "Just to the end of your driveway."

"All right." And she stepped up to move behind Isabelle, who had already taken her place on the scooter.

Chapter Seven

Isabelle tried to convince Cindy to let her go halfway up the driveway when they reached the end, but Cindy shook her head.

"I don't think it's a good idea."

"Yes, but what if she thinks you have

been wasting time in town?"

Cindy was shaking her head before Isabelle finished her question. "She won't when I tell her I was waiting at the dressmaker's until closing."

"What if she does not believe you?"

Cindy laughed at her friend's insistence. "It's a chance I'll have to take." She turned to look toward the house. There were several windows brightly lit.

"I'm sure the girl at the shop will tell her when they go in for their fitting." She shrugged. "If she asks."

Then she turned back to Isabelle. "Now don't you need to get home, too?"

Isabelle nodded and leaned in to give her friend a hug. "I suppose so."

When they separated, she asked, "Do you think everything is going to be all right?"

"Sure." Cindy shrugged again. "What's she gonna do, give me more to do?"

Isabelle laughed. Cindy smiled, knowing how likely that was. Then they hugged again and Cindy stepped back to let Isabelle get back on her scooter.

A minute later, as she watched her friend's scooter roll silently down the narrow lane that led to their driveway, Cindy thought about the differences in her and her friend's lives.

Isabelle's parents were very focused on her education.

Which is why it's a very good thing Isabelle likes to study so much.

Isabelle lived in a nice house in a newer part of the city. She had her own room, with book shelves taking up nearly all of one wall.

What must it be like to have so many books right in your own bedroom?

The books alone would have made Cindy feel like a princess. But Isabelle had her scooter, and she went to one of the most exclusive schools in Silver City. Cindy's step-sisters went there, too, but she went to the local public school.

She did not have her own room, and her stepmother had either donated or sold most of her father's books, using the excuse that they were far too valuable to be read and that Cindy could get whatever books she wanted at the local library.

Cindy was doubly thankful for the library. Not only did she sneak away there as often as possible to read, she had met Isabelle there.

Even with a library all her own at home, Isabelle spent a lot of time at the local library, reading, studying, learning, and discovering new things.

Cindy was usually just happy to find stories to read. She read everything she could get her hands on, including adventure, romance and science fiction or fantasy.

There was nothing better than getting lost inside the pages of a wonderful story, as far as Cindy was concerned.

I certainly inherited Father's love of the written word.

Some of her best memories were of sitting in her father's lap as he read to her. Every time he took a business trip, he returned with new books for them to read together.

Thankfully, Cindy had kept quite a few of those books in her special place in the attic, including some of the most important ones he had brought her.

Those had been safe when her stepmother had started emptying the library.

A few minutes later, Cindy slipped into the house, hoping she could get to her place in the attic without having to run into her stepmother or step-sisters.

Even though she had delivered the list, and the dresses would be ready in time, she knew Isabelle was right.

No one would believe she had been waiting so long to see the dressmaker. They would think she had been wasting her time in town.

And if she slipped, and mentioned anything about the boy who had knocked her down, they would think the worst of that as well.

They would probably think I was lying, that I had met him on purpose and made up the story about him knocking into me so that I could spend time with him and not do chores here.

Chapter Eight

Fortunately she was able to slip up to the attic without anyone seeing her.

When she stepped into the room, being careful to avoid the board just inside the door that creaked so loudly, she was surprised to see a tray sitting on the lumpy old mattress on the floor that served as her bed.

Leesa must have brought my dinner up again.

No easy feat, since climbing the stairs was becoming more difficult for her old nursemaid every day. She did not look forward to the day when her stepmother decided Leesa should retire.

I will miss her so.

She was one of the last links Cindy had to her mother and father. Leesa had served both of her parents, and her, since before she could remember.

A moment later there was a discreet tapping at her door. Cindy moved quickly to open it, avoiding the squeaky board again.

When she opened the door, it was Paulette, their cook and Leesa's granddaughter. She was holding a tray of her own.

When Cindy stepped back to let her in, Paulette spotted the first tray immediately, shaking her head as she set the second one down on the small, broken table beside the bed where Cindy usually stacked the books she was reading.

"She did. I knew it. She came all the way up here."

Cindy turned away to hide her expression. It always amused her to see this young woman, who was not much older than Cindy herself, acting more like her grandmother's keeper than the young person she really was.

She tried to hide her smile. She didn't want Paulette to be upset with her. More than that, she didn't want to have to explain that Leesa's actions were precious to her. Paulette wouldn't understand, but it made Cindy feel more loved than she had in a long while when Leesa took care of her.

Leesa had a lot of trouble with the stairs, but she still found a way to navigate them so she could make sure Cindy did not miss dinner.

She had been taking care of Cindy that way since before she could remember.

Paulette turned quickly back to

where Cindy stood. “Please don't misunderstand. I am glad she brought your dinner up. I just wish she had waited for me.”

She shook her head a little as she said, almost too quietly for Cindy to hear, “I told her I would take care of it.”

Cindy laid a gentle hand on Paulette's arm. “Please don't you be angry with her. Your mother has been taking care of me since forever.”

Paulette nodded, but her voice was sad when she spoke. “I know, and I am glad she's still able for it. I just worry about her.”

“I do, too.” Cindy added.

And that was all they said about the matter. They both worried for Leesa, but there was nothing either of them could do to make her trips upstairs any easier. All they could do was worry. . . and pray for her.

Paulette sat with Cindy and ate the sandwich she had brought. Then she took both trays down to the kitchen while Cindy got ready for bed.

When she knelt beside her bed to say her evening prayers, Cindy went down the list of things and the people she always prayed for.

When she got to Leesa and Paulette, she said an extra little prayer for them both. If anyone was capable of taking the worry from Paulette and the pain from Leesa, it was God.

Chapter Nine

Five days later, Cindy was back at the dressmaker's shop with her stepmother and step-sisters.

Since they had been shopping for most of the morning, she had two armloads worth of bags to carry as well.

The only reason she went in with them was because of the steady drizzle of rain outside. None of them wanted to take a chance on their bags getting soaked.

Cindy stood just inside the store, but far enough away from the trio that she would not have to listen to her step-sisters arguing.

When she spotted the young woman she had spoken to before, she could only nod in greeting. The young woman's face lit up and she waved to Cindy before she even made her way to where Cindy's stepmother stood waiting.

They spoke for only a moment before the young woman disappeared behind a dark curtain.

A few minutes later, she emerged with a dress draped over each arm. Cindy wasn't close enough to hear the conversation, but she could easily imagine it.

When her stepmother moved toward the back of the store and the walls of mirrors, Cindy relaxed, sinking into a thick, comfy chair that was probably intended to be a waiting place for bored husbands.

She was careful to pile the bags around her in the oversized seat so that nothing would be in the way of other customers. Then, she settled in to wait, pulling a book from her shoulder bag.

Sometime later, the young woman appeared in front of Cindy. How long she had stood there waiting to get her attention, Cindy had no idea.

She only knew that a sound distracted her from her reading and she looked up to see the young woman standing there in front of her.

"Good book?" The grin on her face told Cindy she had indeed been standing there for several minutes at least.

Cindy answered truthfully. "It is." She was grateful the young woman didn't look too annoyed with her. . . like her stepmother would have been.

"So, where's your dress? Or did you not want a new one?"

Cindy was surprised to say the least. Not only had the girl remembered her from nearly a week ago, she had remembered that Cindy had no dress ordered.

She debated for a moment about what to say in reply. Then she realized, the truth would be best and the easiest answer.

"Oh. I'm not getting a new dress." It was the truth, just not really all of it, but there was no way Cindy was going to tell the cheerful young woman in front of her that she had never had a new dress in her life. . . at least not in the life she remembered since her father had died.

There was no way she would get to go to this event at the palace. She knew that. She never went to the special events at the palace or anywhere else her stepmother was invited.

"So, what does the dress you're wearing look like, then?"

Cindy opened her mouth to answer, but since she had no idea what to actually say, she closed it again without having made a sound.

The girl waited there for nearly a minute before something finally made it obvious to her that Cindy was not going to the upcoming party.

"I'm sorry. I just. . ." She lifted both hands in a gesture of confusion or helplessness. . . Cindy couldn't be sure. But then, she narrowed her eyes a bit. "Aren't you a bit young to be a servant?"

Cindy nodded. It was all she could do not to laugh now. She was definitely too young, but servant was so clearly the best description for her role in the family, she nodded, then answered as well.

"I would be too young, yes, but I'm not really a servant, either. Well, not in the traditional sense. I'm supposed to be a member of the family, but. . ." It was her turn to shrug helplessly.

How did one properly explain the family she shared a residence with, but nothing else? How could she truly define her role in the family?

She couldn't—not really.

Chapter Ten

Cindy winced at the sudden shrieks that could be heard all the way to the front of the shop.

Clearly Madeline had found fault with the dressmaker's work.

The young woman who had been

waiting for an answer from Cindy, turned and rushed toward the sounds of Madeline's displeasure.

Cindy stayed right where she was. Far too often she had been at the mercy of her step-sister's moods. She knew the safest place to be was far away from the fray.

It was several minutes before the young woman rushed back from the fitting area, a dress laid over her arms and a look of terror on her face.

The poor girl looked as if she were ready to cry. Cindy knew all too well how Madeline enjoyed being difficult to people, for no other reason than it amused her.

Cindy knew that look all too well. And

even though she told herself to stay out of it, she couldn't seem to stop the words from rushing from her. "Is there anything I can do to help?"

"Oh, could you?" The raw hope on the girl's face was more than enough to tell Cindy she was doing the right thing.

Abandoning the small mountain of bags, Cindy moved over to where the young woman sat, the dress in her lap while she worked something into place on the collar.

When Cindy stepped up beside her, she held out the dress a little. "If there was any way you could just hold this for me. . . sewing this into the neckline is impossible to do with it on the form." She held up a thin strip of some sort of lace as she explained.

Cindy took the dress and held it carefully, moving it just a little as the young woman carefully stitched the lace all around the top opening.

They sat there in a comfortable silence for several minutes, one stitching, while the other was holding and moving the material as the sewing continued, before Cindy finally spoke.

“I feel so silly sitting here in silence. Can you talk while you do that or does it need your full attention?”

The young woman laughed a little as she answered. “I can talk and sew at the same time.”

“Oh, good.” Cindy smiled when the young woman looked up at her. “I was just thinking that I've talked to you several times now and I don't even know your name."

"Oh, right!" She disentangled one hand, offering it to Cindy in the age-old greeting. "I'm Piper."

A moment later, she added, "And you're Cindy, right?"

"Right. It's nice to officially meet you."

"You, too."

Cindy waited a few seconds before launching into the apology she had been thinking about since she'd heard Madeline's shriek.

"I am sorry about my step-sister. She's. . ." Cindy stopped, searching for the right word to describe Madeline, seeking a word that would not get her in trouble. “Well, she's used to getting what she wants.”

The young woman beside her made a little sound that was somewhere between a huff and a laugh. “Yeah, I could tell. Wait, did you say step-sister?”

Cindy nodded.

“Well, I suppose that explains that.” She did not elaborate though, and Cindy was too nervous to ask what she meant.

I mean, do I really even want to know?

The truth was, she didn't. She knew her stepmother and step-sisters didn't treat her like family, but hearing about things they said or did was sometimes almost more than Cindy could bear.

It was less than a minute before the stitching stopped and Cindy was helping Piper smooth out the dress where it had gotten a bit crinkled in their handling.

"Thank you. You are a lifesaver. That would have taken me twice as long if I'd had to do it alone." She smiled as she stood, the dress held carefully between them.

Cindy smiled back. "I was happy to help."

She looked the dress over. The color was nothing like she would ever want to wear and the style was much too revealing for her taste, but it was made of such a fine material, she was certain Madeline would look stunning in it.

Even if it was not at all her style, it

was a beautiful dress. Whoever had made it had done a wonderful job.

"It really is a beautiful dress, very well made."

Color filled Piper's cheeks, and Cindy wondered if she were the one who had made the dress, and not her mentor.

That would be quite impressive indeed.

"Thank you. I'm so glad you think so."

Surprise was foremost in Cindy's thoughts, followed by admiration. Anyone who could make something so beautiful was indeed talented.

"Well, I had better get this back to them." Piper smiled again before turning back towards the fitting area of the store.

Cindy watched as Piper walked away, secretly hoping she would have an excuse to stop in again.

It would be nice to have a friend in Piper, and someday, if she could manage to scrape together enough money somehow, she would love to ask Piper to make her a dress.

Chapter Eleven

The night of the party arrived and Cindy found herself helping her step-sisters prepare for it.

She forced herself to smile as she tied laces, tucked up loose curls and provided a brace for pushing feet into shoes that were obviously a bit too tight.

When the front bell announced the arrival of a limousine, she even stood on the front stoop and waved to them.

Then she turned to go back inside, thinking how nice it would be to curl up with a good book and read all evening, for certainly it would be late before her stepmother and step-sisters returned home.

She had made it halfway up the stairs when the bell rang again. Thinking one of them must have forgotten something, she turned to run back down and see what needed fetching.

However, the sight that greeted her at the door was not at all what... or who she was expecting.

Standing on the front stoop were her best friend in the whole world and the young woman from the dressmaker's shop.

Behind Isabelle and the young dressmaker's apprentice was another long limousine. Piper held up a dress that was positively stunning.

Isabelle took her hand and pulled her back through the house. “Come on. We don't have much time. We're going to be late!” And then she was pulling Cindy up the stairs.

It took Cindy several long moments to realize they had stopped in her step-sister's room, and that Isabelle was already dressed for the party.

She pushed Cindy down to the chair by Madeline's wide vanity. "We have to get you ready."

When Cindy looked into the mirror, she saw that Piper had slipped into the room at some point and that she was dressed for the party as well.

She held up the dress Cindy had seen earlier and she took a minute now to look at it more closely.

It was made of what looked to be a as fine a material as Madeline and Abigail's dresses had been made from.

It had a full skirt and a much more modest neckline than Madeline's. The color of the underskirt was the most beautiful blue, and the overskirt was a shimmery, nearly translucent white. The sleeves were short, slightly puffed, also using the blue underlay and shimmery overlay.

It looked like something a princess would wear. . . or someone very important—certainly not her.

Finally, Cindy found her voice. "Isabelle, what is going on? How did you do all of this? Why did you do this?"

Isabelle was busy pulling things from the bag she had carried upstairs; a bag Cindy had not even noticed before.

"Cindy, you are my best friend and one of the most intelligent people I know, but that is really a dumb question." She shook her head as she laid items out on Madeline's vanity.

From behind them, Piper giggled.

"Don't you get it, Cindy? Tonight, Isabelle and I are your fairy godmothers, and it is time you had a chance to go to the ball." She giggled again and gently laid the dress on Madeline's bed, walking over to where Isabelle was starting to apply makeup to Cindy's face.

"I've got shoes, too." She pulled several pairs of shoes out of another bag Cindy hadn't seen her carry inside.

Over the next twenty minutes, Isabelle and Piper transformed Cindy from someone who cleaned for a living into a princess.

Even she was forced to admit, when she looked at the finished product in Madeline's mirror, that she looked nothing like herself.

No one could possibly recognize me in this.

The thought was exciting. She could go to the party and her stepmother and step-sisters would never even realize it was her.

They would never imagine the young woman in a blue dress and tiara was the same girl who cleaned up after them and delivered their breakfast each morning before school.

"But how will I get in? I wasn't invited."

Isabelle only grinned. "You're my plus one, of course." Then she grabbed the bag she must have repacked while Cindy was marveling at her transformation in one hand and took Cindy's hand in her other, and then they were all three quickly racing down the stairs to the waiting limousine.

Chapter Twelve

Atop the hill, the castle stood, lights shining from every window like beacons of hope and welcome.

Cindy leaned as close to the window as she dared, looking at the sight of the castle as their limousine drew closer to it.

She had seen it lit up like this on many occasions, but never so close up. It was absolutely breathtaking.

Beside her, Piper and Isabelle were telling her things she would need to know for the party, like to avoid dark-colored liquids.

They also agreed to a signal that she could send either of them if she needed rescuing.

Then they were at the gates, and Isabelle and Piper were staring just as intently at the palace and the crowds as Cindy was.

“Try to get it all out of your system now. You don't want to look starstruck or anything once we're inside." Piper told her.

"Yeah. Try looking a little bored, if you can." Isabelle spoke with the authority of someone who had attended dozens of these parties. "If you look too excited or in awe, it will draw a lot more attention than you want, trust me."

Cindy nodded, but didn't take her eyes off the sight that was filling the right side of the windows now.

When the car slowed, she took several deep breaths, but there was no calming the speeding of her heart.

Here she had been wishing she could have Piper make her a dress and somehow get to one of the parties at the palace someday, and it was all happening—right now.

"It's just like a fairy tale." She whispered the words. Either Piper and Isabelle didn't hear her, or they were just too entranced by the palace, too, but neither one replied.

When the limousine stopped and a uniformed footman opened the door beside Isabelle, she grinned back at Cindy and Piper before relaxing the muscles in her face, letting her expression turn to one of slight boredom, just like she had told Cindy to do.

Then she was out of the car, and the footman held out a hand to Cindy, which she gratefully accepted. Her dress was much more to maneuver in than she would have thought.

She tried to relax her own face, and look slightly bored, like Isabelle had done, but there was so much to look at as they walked in, following a long line of men, women, and teenagers all dressed in their finest.

When they walked into the main ballroom, Cindy was careful to stay a step behind Isabelle and Piper, so she could follow their lead.

They followed the crowd, but once inside the ballroom, both girls were offered a young man's arm and they looked back at her with a smile, heading off to enjoy the party.

Then she was on her own.

Determined to enjoy herself, she

moved slowly around the enormous room, looking at everything as she made her way to the long tables at one side of the room that held several different kinds of drink and more snack foods than she had ever seen in one place before.

They were arranged a little outside the main ballroom, under a wide set of archways and there were attendants every few feet to pour drinks and place treats on plates.

Cindy picked one of the drinks that was clear and wandered back out towards the main area where couples were already dancing.

"Well, fancy seeing you here." The voice by Cindy's ear was oddly familiar and she turned to see who it belonged to.

Standing behind her was the boy who had knocked her down the week before. He was leaning against a pillar looking quite bored. Something in his behavior told her he was not faking it.

Surprised, not only to see him there, but that he had recognized her, she took a moment to look him over.

He too was dressed in finery, but he wore it like—a prince. His hair still had a hint of messiness to it, but it had mostly been tamed, and though he was leaning against the pillar, his posture was absolutely perfect.

Watching her watching him, the crooked grin of his appeared suddenly and he pushed away from the pillar, holding out a hand to her.

"Would you like to dance?"

She could only nod as she put her hand in his and let him lead her out onto the dance floor. He didn't stop until they had reached the center.

As he turned to face her, he bent slightly forward in a bow, before reaching for her hand as the music began.

Recognizing the dance, and breathing a sigh of relief that it happened to be one of the few they were all required to learn in school, Cindy curtsied in return, before moving her other hand up to his shoulder.

Then they were moving together

across the dance floor. It seemed almost as if they were flying at times.

Cindy knew for certain that this was the best night she would ever have. . . and one she would never, ever forget!

This is NOT the end. . .

It's just the beginning!

"His lord said unto him, Well done, good and faithful servant; thou hast been faithful over a few things, I will make thee ruler over many things; enter thou into the joy of thy Lord."

~ Matthew 25:23

A NOTE FROM MACY

Magic, wondrous characters, and fantastical stories are only a few of the things I love about Fairy Tales.

And, as much as I love the originals, I love making new stories for the beloved characters we've all grown up with.

I hope readers who enjoy Fairy Tales as much as I do, will enjoy the modern twists my mother and I have added to these much-loved stories.

~ Macy

"For God so loved the world, that He gave His only begotten Son, that whosoever believeth in Him should not perish, but have everlasting life."

~ John 3:16

A NOTE FROM JC

Like most little girls with fanciful imaginations, I have always had a special place in my heart for Fairy tales.

Who doesn't love a world where villains get what's coming to them, good always wins, and little girls are rewarded the truest desires of their hearts in the end?

We don't live in a world where many people get the desires of their hearts, nor a world where good and evil always come out where they should.

That is one reason I write fantasy that follows this all-important formula. We all need that safe place.

~ JC

"Call unto me, and I will answer thee,
and shew thee great and mighty things,
which thou knowest not."
~ Jeremiah 33:3

ABOUT THE AUTHORS

Macy Morrows is a young girl following in her mother's footsteps, with storytelling, having her head in the clouds, and spending her time in fictional worlds. She fits in better than her mother ever did though. . . and that's not a bad thing

JC Morrows is an author of fantastical fiction filled with faith. She writes about assassins, aliens, dragons, angels, fairy tales, and teenagers trying desperately to survive in post-apocalptic worlds.

She also drinks coffee. . . lots and lots of coffee.

ABOUT THE PUBLISHER

Christian Publishing for HIS GLORY

S&G Publishing offers books with messages that honor Jesus Christ to the world! S&G works with Christian authors to bring you the best in "inspirational" fiction and non-fiction.

S&G is proud to publish a variety of Christian fiction genres:
inspirational romance
young reader
young adult
speculative
historical
suspense

Check out our website at:
sgpublish.com

DON'T MISS BOOK TWO

WELCOME TO SILVER CITY: WHERE HAPPILY EVER AFTER IS STILL A MODERN GIRL'S DREAM!

Maree is not your average girl. She rides, climbs trees, is an expert archer, and a constant embarrassment to her very proper mother.

If only she could have been born a boy... like her three rambunctious younger brothers... who can do no wrong in their parents' eyes...

BOOK TWO OF THE SILVER CITY PRINCESS STORIES

MORE FROM JC & MACY

As if being a teenager isn't hard enough. . .

Can you imagine how it feels to wake up one day and find out that you are not who you thought you were?

If you're anything like me, you know it's hard enough trying to fit in—in high school—without having to deal with the knowledge that your dad is an alien part of the time. I don't even get how you can be an alien part of the time...

As if I don't have enough to deal with. . .

It's crazy enough to find out, the hard way, that you are not who you thought you were.

But to have that kind of bombshell dropped on you, and then — to have your Dad ditch you — leaving you to figure stuff out all by yourself, with a Mom you can't tell anything about what's going on. . .

MORE FROM S&G Publishing

SOPHIE IS A KITTEN WHO FOUND TWO CHILDREN . . . AND DECIDED TO ADOPT THEM AS HER OWN

Read along with Sammy and Macy as they tell the story of finding a little lost kitten, naming her, loving her, and making her part of their (or rather, becoming her own) family.

Enjoy Thanksgiving with them. Read about how Sophie celebrates this fun holiday filled with food, family and mischief.

Then read about how Sophie's family made the move from the big city... and Sophie followed.

Now she has her own house, a big yard, and new kitty friends right next door!

Katie Chupp spends her days at The Sweet Shop, taking care of customers and baking delicious treats... not exactly a profession where one expects to be thrown into the midst of mysteries and mayhem.

But when the bakery is broken into, someone has to find the thief . . . besides finding another place to do the baking and get the orders to the customers.

Is this a random theft, or is the thief trying to ruin the town's Independence Day celebration?

It's the most wonderful time of the year and Katie Chupp is spending her days catering to the holiday rush. With everyone in town ordering special desserts and treats, will Katie be able to find time to finish making gifts for her family and friends?

With a winter chill settling in and Christmas right around the corner, no one would expect a mystery, but a mystery does indeed appear... And this is one mystery that may never be solved...

Amelia Simpkins may be a great cook, and have a head for business, but sweet treats are out of her league and the owner of the Irish Blessings Cafe says it's because she adds the tart to the Sweet Shop's new dessert that Katie Chupp insists is only filled with lemony goodness.

The two shop owners' constant bickering sends sparks flying through Abbott Creek's usual calm... and when Andrew's cafe suffers from some rather unusual pest problems, the town starts taking sides.

It's the time of year when the residents of Abbott Creek give thanks for their blessings.

But Katie is having difficulty deciding whether she should be thankful. . . or careful of the new relationships she has developed over the previous year...

Katie Chupp is not the only person in Abbott Creek looking forward to the most romantic holiday of the year...

But Valentine's Day will not be all hearts and flowers. There are secrets to be kept, feelings to be explored, and difficult decisions to be made — and each one has something to do with the heart.

Will those secrets come between friends? Will the happy couples in Abbott Creek get to celebrate. . . together?

Between babies and budding romances, busy schedules and unexpected gossip, the small town and its residents may never be the same.

Everyone at the Sweet Shop Bakery and the Irish Blessings cafe is worrying over Bella and her baby – and busily trying to convince her to take it easy.

Katie is not the only person in town with some big decisions ahead of her. And the busy summer season is kicked off with a big surprise for everyone.

www.ingramcontent.com/pod-product-compliance
Lightning Source LLC
Chambersburg PA
CBHW070444170726
48291CB00005B/1597

* 9 7 8 1 9 4 8 7 3 3 9 4 6 *